Violett Valentine

By Heidi Herschbach

With gratitude to the real Gramma Marge.
Thank you for the world, the music,
and the hunger for adventure.

For Miss P. Valentine, the bravest of girls, may you
always shine so brightly my darling.
And for Gailybug, without you nothing would have been.
You are both so loved.

Thank you Literary Aunties!

May all of the "Violetts" of the world follow
their dreams, seek adventure,
and spread kindness.

Violett Valentine by Heidi Herschbach
Published by Violett Valentine LLC.
P.O. Box 2612, Portland, OR

violettvalentine.com

Cover by Heidi Herschbach

Ebook ISBN: 978-1-64255-993-4

Her name is Violett Valentine.

Her passport is wearing thin.

"I have a zany accent from
the places that I've been."

Her suitcase is overflowing,
so she packs it with her feet.

She's walking down the aisle
and she's looking for her seat.

Gramma Marge and Violett travel
all around the world.

The sights they see inspire them to sew for boys and girls.

Violett has a buddy that she brings along with her,
a three toed sloth named Jerry, with wild tangled fur.

Trend setter, jet setter, sketching as she goes.
Daydreamer playing music, twirling on her toes.

Violett and her Gramma Marge
are on their way to Greece,
to see the ancient ruins
and meet Violett's Aunt Bernice.

After they have landed,
the pilot bids "Good Day."

Aunt Bernice is there to pick
them up and start their holiday.

The Acropolis sits high above the city on a rock.
They hike their way up to the top, a very dusty walk.
It used to be a fortress, it holds the Parthenon;
a very famous building, a greek phenomenon.

The pillars tall and vertical, the bases curved and round,
Caryatids* dressed in tunics that pool upon the ground.

*Caryatids are sculptures of females that hold up buildings or architectural structures.

Inside of the museum are findings very rare,
statues of the Grecian people, works of art to share.

Plaka* is on rick-rack streets that wind this way and that.

*Plaka is a very famous old neighborhood/area in Athens that sits at the bottom of the slopes of the Acropolis.

Downhill from the Acropolis, each doorway has a cat.

Violett spies two kids her age,
she loves to meet the locals.
"Howdy kids, I have a fiddle!
I'll play and you do vocals!"

The children are not singing as she sings and plays the song.
Instead they snicker, point and whisper.

"Guess I don't belong."
Violett feels embarassed, she's hurt and says goodbye.
The kids attempt to stop her, she's trying not to cry.

"Let's be speedy, taxi's here. Violett, please don't dawdle."
Aunt Bernice is nibbling nuts, she has a hurried waddle.
"Please one moment, Aunt Bernice,
my knapsack sure feels light."
Violett's face goes pale, Jerry's gone, nowhere in sight.

Jerry's tie is on the ground.
"Thank goodness, it's a clue!"

"Kýrios, have you seen a sloth?
Please, any news will do."
She shows the man a photo
of Jerry recently.
"They went that way!" He points downhill.
"The boat sets sail at three."

"Come on Chickpeas, follow me!" Bernice lets out a snort.
"I know the way, we'll rescue him.
Now onward to the port."
They're off to Santorini on a giant ferry boat.
Our friend Jerry will be brave,
as you know, sloths can float.

The buildings are so vibrant, blue roofs against stark white.
Poor donkeys carry tourists uphill with all their might.

Outside of little windows, string underpants and socks.
The plaster walls so crumbly showcase the locals frocks.

After looking high and low, before they leave for Crete,
she spots the kids from Athens swinging Jerry by his feet.
"Hello again, I see you have the sloth which I have lost.
Please gently hand him back to me,
his value's beyond cost."

The children start to giggle,
they toss him in the air.
Jerry looks concerned,
wind ruffles up his hair.

"Unhand him, trouble makers!
Your plan is now kaput.
Shall I contact the Embassy,
and call the guards afoot?"

"You hurt my feelings,
took my sloth,
you snickered at my song."

The kids are feeling sheepish.

"Making fun of you was wrong.
As for Jerry Sloth you see,
we found him on the ground.
We're sorry that we threw him."

"I'm so grateful he's been found!"

Hugging Jerry tightly, Violett says she understands.
"Thank you friends, this means so much!"
The three of them shake hands.

After saying their goodbyes, a Grecian feast awaits.
The Santorini sun is setting; it's time for breaking plates*!

*Breaking plates is a tradition at celebratory ceremonies (such as weddings) and also funerals, although not as common anymore.

The waiter brings out Saganaki*, olives, pita bread.
Violett tries to sneak away, a napkin on her head.

*Pan fried brined white/goat cheese served as an appetizer.

"My dear, you simply
have to sample
such a fragrant cheese.
Unless you have an allergy
.... I didn't hear you sneeze."

"Opa!" Violett celebrates.
Quite thankful that she tried.
The chef peaks from the kitchen
and he's beaming, full of pride.

"One last picture!" Gramma says.
"Bernice! Your eyes were closed!
Everybody lookey here!"

Jerry and Violett stay posed.

Aunt Bernice is teary eyed, she's smooching one and all.
"Antio sas." They say a Greek goodbye.
"Please don't forget to call!"

Thank you friends for joining us,
this is the ending rhyme.
With Gramma Marge and Jerry Sloth,
please join us all next time.

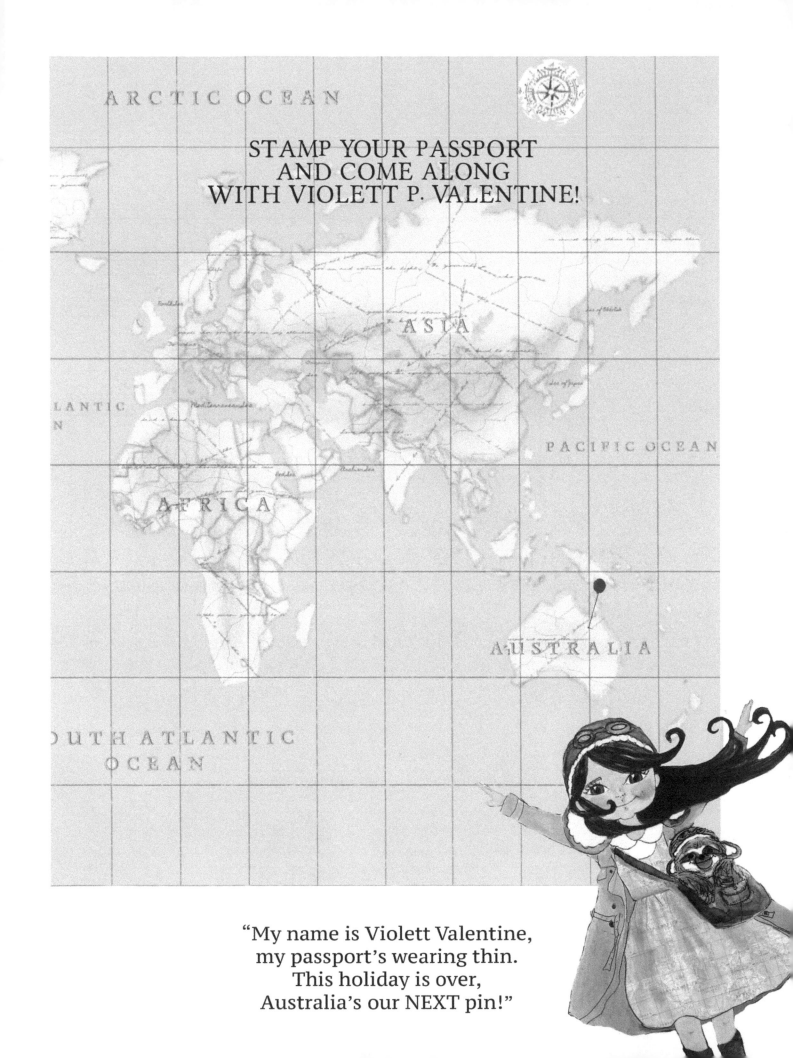

STAMP YOUR PASSPORT
AND COME ALONG
WITH VIOLETT P. VALENTINE!

"My name is Violett Valentine,
my passport's wearing thin.
This holiday is over,
Australia's our NEXT pin!"

Aunt Bernice's Baklava recipe

1 (16oz) pkg. phyllo dough
1 pound chopped nuts
1 c. butter
1.5 tsp. ground cinnamon
1 c. water
1 c. cane sugar
2 tsp. vanilla extract
3/4 c. honey

1. Preheat oven to 350 degrees
butter sides and bottom of 9x13" pan
2. choop nuts and toss with cinnamon.
place two sheets of dough in pan and butter.
Repeat until you have 8 sheets layered.
Sprinkle 2-3 tablespoons of nut mixture on top.
then layer two sheets dough, butter, nuts, and
keep layering until its 6-8 layers deep.
3. Cut into squares through all layers.
Bake for 50 min. until crisp and golden.
4. While baklava is baking, boil sugar and
water until sugar is melted. Add
vanilla and honey, simmer 20 min.
5. Remove baklava from oven and spoon
sauce over it right away. Let cool. Serve.
Enjoy chickpeas!
Love Aunt Bernice

VIOLETT'S
notes from lunch
- Blue and gray/white
checked fabric
like table cloth

- Key pattern like
on plates
- lemons from food,
- Colors from food,
plates and table cloth
(blue, white, yellow, green
gray, red, orange

10 EURO

CPSIA information can be obtained
at www.ICGtesting.com
Printed in the USA
BVHW02*1428120718
521342BV00007B/28/P